To the Slote Soccer Squad—
Karen and Jon, Lindsay and Nina,
and Oliver, too!
—S.J.M.

For my awe-inspiring nieces, Emily, Laura, Marcie,
Enrica, Fiona, and Onotse. Love is the goal.
—C.L.J.

The publisher and author would like to thank
teachers Patricia Chase, Phyllis Goldman, and
Patrick Hopfensperger for their help in making
the math in MathStart just right for kids.

HarperCollins®, ♠®, and MathStart® are registered trademarks of HarperCollins Publishers.
For more information about the MathStart series, write to
HarperCollins Childre's Books, 10 East 53rd Street, New York, NY 10022.
or visit our web site at www.harperchildrens.com.

Bugs incorporated in the MathStart series design were painted by Jon Buller.

Game Time!
Text copyright © 2000 by Stuart J. Murphy
Illustrations copyright © 2000 by Cynthia Jabar
Manufactured in China. All rights reserved.

Library of Congress Cataloging-in-Publication Data
Murphy, Stuart J., 1942—
    Game time! / by Stuart J. Murphy ; illustrated by Cynthia Jabar.
        p.   cm.
    Summary: Calendars and clocks keep track of passing time as the Huskies prepare for
and compete in the championship soccer game against the Falcons.
    ISBN 0-06-028024-7. — ISBN 0-06-028025-5 (lib. bdg.)
    ISBN 0-06-446732-5 (pbk.)
    [1. Soccer—Fiction.   2. Time—Fiction.   3. Clocks and watches—Fiction.]
I. Jabar, Cynthia, ill.   II. Title.
PZ7.M9563Gam   2000   98-51902
[Fic]—dc21   CIP
                                                  AC

Typography by Elynn Cohen
11 12 13 SCP 30 29 28 27 26 25 24
❖

GAME TIME!

wish us luck.

by Stuart J. Murphy · illustrated by Cynthia Jabar

HARPERCOLLINSPUBLISHERS

MathStart TIME

LEVEL 3

Just before practice on Saturday, a group of girls passed by the soccer field and yelled out, "Two, four, six, eight! Who do we think is really great? The Falcons!"

Maria, Rebecca, and Ashley were heading to the locker room with Oliver. They yelled back, "Huskies! Huskies! We're the best! We're gonna put you to the test!"

The big soccer game between the Falcons and the Huskies was just one week away. Last year the Falcons were the league champions. "We can beat them this year!" said Rebecca. "Then *we'll* be the champions!"

"We have the best mascot," said Ashley as she gave Oliver a big hug.

"It's already October 7th," said Maria. "We only have 7 more days. We'll have to practice really hard."

All week long the Huskies practiced dribbling, passing, and scoring. Oliver came to every practice. Finally it was Friday. The championship game was just 1 day away.

"Don't worry," said Rebecca. "In 24 hours the game will be over and we'll be league champs!"

"Right, Oliver?" said Ashley.

"Woof!" agreed Oliver.

On Saturday morning Rebecca, Ashley and Maria hurried down to the soccer field to meet Coach Russo and the rest of the team. Oliver came with them.

They got there at 9 o'clock and the game started at 10.
They had an hour to warm up.

The Falcons were already there. They looked tough.
They looked good. They looked *really* good.

"In 60 minutes we'll be Falcon food," Maria moaned.

After both teams had stretched and warmed up, Jake, the referee, arrived. It was 10 o'clock.

Jake looked at his watch and yelled,

"GAME TIME!"

Both teams were ready for the kickoff. Oliver galloped up and down the sidelines.

The two teams dribbled and passed the ball up and down the field for almost a quarter of an hour. No one scored. Then one of the Falcons broke away and ran for the goal.

Maria did her best to block the goal, but it was too late. The Falcons scored the first goal. Jake blew his whistle, and the first period was over. Already 15 minutes had gone by.

Just 5 minutes into the second period, a teammate
passed the ball to Rebecca. With a quick kick
Rebecca sent the ball flying past the Falcon goalie.

There were 2 minutes to go in the second period. One of the Falcons got the ball again. It was almost halftime. They had been playing for nearly 30 minutes. Ashley tried to steal the ball back. But the Falcon kicked it past her, right into the goal.

Teams	Score	GAME TIME LEFT
FALCONS	2	**30:00**
HUSKIES	1	min sec

"Halftime!" Jake yelled.
Half an hour was gone, and the
score was Falcons 2, Huskies 1.

½ hour =
30 minutes

The two teams ran off the field for a 15-minute break.

While they rested and drank lots of water, Coach Russo gave everyone orange slices to eat. He even had a dog biscuit for Oliver.

"They've got us beat," Maria said, sighing. "We'll never get to be champions."

"We can still do it," said Rebecca. "Remember our cheer?"
"Huskies! Huskies! We're the best! We're gonna put you
to the test!" the whole team shouted. Oliver barked along.

Teams | score | GAME TIME LEFT
FALCONS | 2 | 30:00
HUSKIES | 1 | min   sec

"Your 15 minutes are up!" hollered Jake. They rushed back onto the field.

You can do it!

21

Both teams were playing good defense, and 15 minutes passed without a goal. Oliver watched from the sidelines.

45 minutes = 3/4 hour

Jake blew his whistle to announce
that the third period was over.
They had been playing for 45
minutes, and the Falcons were
still in the lead.

As the fourth period began, Rebecca yelled, "This is our last chance!"

"Go, Huskies, go!" Ashley shouted.

Oliver barked and barked. For most of the period no one could score. Then Ashley got the ball and headed it to Rebecca.

Rebecca turned, got the ball, and kicked it right
into the goal.

"Tied game," yelled Jake. "There's 1 minute to go."

The Falcons had the ball again, but Rebecca rushed in and stole it. She took off down the field. Already 45 seconds of the last minute were gone.

Coach Russo ran to the sidelines. The crowd counted down the seconds as Rebecca ran: "15, 14, 13, 12 . . ."

Rebecca got ready to kick the ball, but suddenly a Falcon blocked her shot. There was no way she could make the goal!

"11, 10, 9 . . ." the crowd yelled.

Quickly Rebecca passed the ball to Maria. And Maria kicked it into the Falcons' net to score!

"Huskies win! Huskies win!" cheered the team.
The Huskies shook hands with the Falcons and then charged off the field.
The Huskies were finally the champs!

In *Game Time!*, the math concept is time. To measure time we use units like weeks, days, hours, minutes, and seconds. The relationships between these units, as well as how clocks and calendars represent them, are important concepts for children to master.

If you would like to have more fun with the math concepts presented in *Game Time!*, here are a few suggestions:

- Read the story together and ask the child to make a list of the ways time is measured (weeks, days, hours, minutes, and seconds).

- As you reread the story have the child note the relationships between various units of time. For example, 1 week = 7 days.

- Have the child make a list of four events that happened in his or her day and the time that each occurred. Have the child draw four clocks, one for each time.

- Ask the child to close his or her eyes and then open them when he or she thinks one minute has passed. Check the difference between the estimate and the actual elapsed time. Try this with other family members or friends. Compare the child's estimate with others'.

- Together, count the number of half hours, quarter hours, and minutes in an hour. Repeat the activity with a two-hour block of time.

- Circle the child's birthday on a calendar. Ask how many months, weeks, and days until this date.

1 day = 24 hours

Following are some activities that will help you extend the concepts presented in *Game Time!* into a child's everyday life.

Around the House: How many kinds of clocks can you find at home? Can you find a watch, a wall clock, a stopwatch, an alarm clock, a clock on an oven or microwave? How are all the clocks the same? How are they different?

Cooking: Make a cake with the child. Note how long the cake needs to bake and the time the cake is placed in the oven. At various intervals ask the child how much time is left before the cake is done. When the remaining time is less than one minute, ask how many seconds are left. After the cake is done, guess how many seconds it will take to eat a piece!

Chores: Before doing a chore such as cleaning a bedroom, have the child predict how long the activity will take. For chores that take less than a minute, like drying a glass, predict the duration in seconds. Time the chore, then check to see how close the estimate was.

The following books include some of the same concepts that are presented in *Game Time!*

* THE GROUCHY LADYBUG by Eric Carle

* TIME TO . . . by Bruce McMillan

* TUESDAY by David Wiesner